10-19

BL   AR pts

Same Way Ben

Maryann Cocca-Leffler

Albert Whitman & Company
Chicago, Illinois

To Poppy and Brody——
wishing you a lifetime of adventure!
Love, Auntie Maryann

Library of Congress Cataloging-in-Publication data is on file with the publisher.

Text and illustrations copyright © 2019 by Maryann Cocca-Leffler
First published in the United States of America in 2019 by Albert Whitman & Company
ISBN 978-0-8075-7222-1 (hardcover)
ISBN 978-0-8075-7223-8 (ebook)

Printed in China
10 9 8 7 6 5 4 3 2 1 HH 24 23 22 21 20 19

Visit Maryann at www.MaryannCoccaLeffler.com.
For more information about Albert Whitman & Company,
visit our website at www.albertwhitman.com.

100 Years of Albert Whitman & Company
Celebrate with us in 2019!

Ben liked things the same way—every day.

When Ben dressed for
school, he always wore
his favorite overalls with
his red striped shirt.

When he got off the bus, his teacher,
Mrs. Garcia, always patted his head and said,

Ben sat at the same green table with his best friend, Cami.

And he always ate chicken strips and a shiny apple for lunch.

Life was the same every day. Until...

Ben looked up. It was Mr. Elliot, the music teacher.
Ben didn't like to be called Benjamin.
If Mrs. Garcia were here, she would know that.

In the classroom, Mr. Elliot made an announcement.

"I will be your teacher for the next six weeks. Mrs. Garcia had her baby. It's a boy. His name is Brody."

Everyone cheered, except Ben.

Next, Mr. Elliot passed out paper and paints.
He played loud music.

"Listen to the music and paint what
you hear," he told the class.

"Mrs. Garcia never plays music
in the morning," said Ben. "We
always have reading time first."

"Benjamin, today we are
changing things up," said
Mr. Elliot.

Ben didn't like music in the morning.

If Mrs. Garcia were here, she would know that.

But Ben still sat at the same green table,

played with his best friend, Cami,

and ate chicken strips for lunch.

Life was *almost*
the same every day.

Until...

it wasn't.

On Monday, Mr. Elliot moved all the tables around.
Cami went to sit at the yellow table.

"Mrs. Garcia never moves the tables,"
said Ben. "The green table is always in the
corner near the cubbies."

"Benjamin, today we are changing things up," said Mr. Elliot.

But Ben didn't like when the tables were moved.

If Mrs. Garcia were here, she would know that.

"We're having some special guests for lunch," said Mr. Elliot. "I made us blueberry and cream cheese bagels to share."

Ben just stood in the middle of the classroom.

He didn't know what to do,
or where to sit,
or what to eat.

Suddenly he said...

My name is NOT Benjamin!
I want to sit with Cami
at the GREEN table!
I want chicken strips and
an apple for lunch!
and... and...
I WANT MRS. GARCIA!

Ben began to cry.

Just then he felt a pat on his head.

"MRS. GARCIA!
You're HERE!"
"I'm just visiting for lunch
today. I wanted the class to
meet Brody."

"Mrs. Garcia, I miss you," Ben said. "Nothing is the same. Mr. Elliot is changing everything."

Mrs. Garcia leaned in. "Can I tell you a secret? My new baby changed everything for me."

"He did?" Ben asked.

"But guess what?" said Mrs. Garcia. "Changes make life exciting...like an adventure!"

Mrs. Garcia noticed Ben's painting on the board.

"Ben, is this yours? It's beautiful."

"We painted to music," said Ben.

"Well, we never did that before," said Mrs. Garcia. "And you are becoming a very good artist!"

"I am?" Ben looked at his painting and smiled.

Mrs. Garcia handed Ben a bagel. "Let's have lunch together."
Ben took a nibble. Then a larger bite, and then he ate the whole thing.

"I didn't know you liked blueberry and cream cheese bagels," Mrs. Garcia said.

"I didn't know either," said Ben.

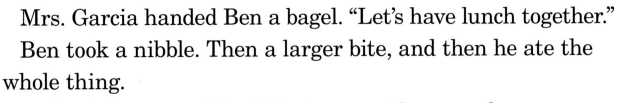

The next day Ben wore his
favorite overalls with a blue shirt,

sat at the yellow table with
his friends Cami and Poppy,

and ate pizza for lunch.

And before he knew it, Mrs. Garcia was back for good.

But for Ben, life was never the same...
it was an adventure.